# CONTENTS

*For Line, my favourite neighbour*

*JM*

*To Harvey*

*DH*

*For Jon*

*CE*

# Chapter 1

# Mrs Potter's great Idea

I'm Arthur and I'm seven, and the other day, when I was with my grandfather at Picket Lake, I found a dog; a big, hairy, grey and white dog. Since he looked lost, and he was really nice, we took him home.

"You must find out who this dog belongs to!" said my grandmother.

She was right.

Grandad and I went off to visit all the neighbours, and took the dog with us. But nobody recognised him. And nobody wanted him either. So we had no choice…

We took him back to Grandma.

"Can he stay?" I asked.

"Absolutely not!" Grandma replied.

"Pleeeeeeease? Just for tonight?"

"I know what you're like, Arthur. Just one night together and the two of you will be inseparable. You've already done the same thing to us with that duck of yours."

I promised not to get too attached to the dog. Grandad promised, too. And the big dog was allowed to spend one night with us.

But when I woke up the next morning, the house was quiet. The dog wasn't there. Nor was Grandma.

"Look outside," said Grandad, smiling.

Out in the garden, the dog was doing its best to entertain Grandma. He was bringing back all the sticks she was throwing. It looked like the two of them were getting on well. Grandad, my duck and I went out to join them.

"Why don't you just adopt him?" asked Mrs Potter, the lady who lived next door, who was spying on us over the hedge.

"It's always sensible to have a good guard dog around, to keep an eye on things."

"Not on your life!" replied Grandma. "We're already keeping Arthur's duck, and that's more than enough."

"But burglars aren't scared of ducks!"

"And burglars don't come to Picket Lake," explained Grandad.

Mrs Potter rushed around the hedge. She charged towards my grandfather and said:

"Burglars are like chickenpox, Geoffrey Franklin. You never know when they're going to show up!"

"I think he'd be a brilliant guard dog," I added, stroking him.

"Finally, I'll be able to sleep soundly," muttered Mrs Potter, as she made her way back round the hedge.

My grandmother didn't reply. She went back to the house with a very serious expression on her face. Grandad, the dog, my duck and I followed her.

# Chapter 2

# Eugene's Opinion

A minute later, Grandma was on the phone. I was sure she was calling the Animal Shelter, to ask them to come and collect the dog. That's what Grandad was afraid of, too.

"What are you doing?" asked my grandfather, a little anxiously.

"I'm calling Eugene," she told us, dialling my cousin's number. "He'll give us good advice about this dog."

"Does Cousin Eugene know about dogs?" I asked.

"Eugene has been to university. I'm sure he will know whether or not this dog might be useful to us."

"What will happen then?"

"We'll see, Arthur. We'll see."

Eugene arrived in the afternoon, with a pile of books that told us all the good things dogs could do. Then Grandma asked the dog to do all kinds of useless tricks, like sitting, lying down, and sitting again.

He was very patient and always did what he was told. Cousin Eugene was impressed.

"We are in the presence of a unique phenomenon!" he declared. "This animal has developed an exceptionally quick bond with you, Aunt Margaret."

"You really think he's talented?" asked Grandma.

"Not him!"

"Huh?"

"You!"

"Me?"

"It's perfectly clear you have a remarkable gift with animals."

"Come now, Eugene."

"This animal will be a loyal guard dog for you, day and night."

"Are you quite sure about what

you're suggesting?" asked Granddad.

"Undoubtedly!" replied Eugene. "With him around, there's no doubt about it. You'll be absolutely safe."

Then I asked the most important question of all.

"So, can he stay, Grandma?"

She looked at the dog, who was snoring on the sofa, and replied:

"We'll see, Arthur. We'll see."

## Chapter 3
# The Big Test

Grandma spent the rest of the day looking through the books that Eugene had brought. They did look very interesting. That evening, she announced that she was going to give her first proper training lesson.

"Come along, dog!" Grandma called out.

Since he was lying with me on the sofa, eating popcorn while watching TV, the dog didn't feel much like working. So he didn't move.

"Come on! Come here!" Grandma called again. "Come here at once!"

"Oh, leave the poor dog alone, Margaret," growled Grandad, who was also watching TV. "It is Saturday, after all."

"What does the dog know about what day it is?" replied Grandma. "And besides, don't forget that very soon he's going to have to take the Big Test. He should really stop watching TV."

The Big Test was Eugene's idea. In order to find out whether the dog was a good guard dog, we would have to pretend that there was a real burglar.

So, that evening, we all went to bed very early, but only so that we could pretend to sleep when the pretend burglar was pretending to do his pretend burglary.

The dog was in the small bedroom with me. As he didn't know that he was going to be taking this Big Test — because no one had explained it to him — he fell asleep for real.

Later that night, I heard strange sounds coming from the garden. I looked out and saw Cousin Eugene. I recognised him even though he was wearing a black balaclava over his head, a torn coat, and yellow rubber gloves for doing the washing-up. His burglar's disguise was really convincing.

Eugene prowled close to the house, around the walls, and looked in the windows, like a thief. As for the dog, he snored peacefully. I gave him a shake to help him a little.

"Wake up, you big lazybones. They're making you do a test."

He opened one eye, and yawned.

"Bark! Growl! Do something!"

He went back to sleep. This had started very badly.

Then I heard a cry; a loud cry coming from the garden.

"Heeeeeeelp!"

It was Eugene's voice.

At once, Grandad and Grandma appeared in my room. We all rushed to the window, and we saw… our neighbour,

Mrs Potter, pursuing our robber, armed with a huge frying pan.

"I haven't stolen anything!" Eugene was saying over and over.

"That's only because I arrived in time!" shouted Mrs Potter, who had no intention of giving up the chase.

Eugene ran off down the little lane. We rushed out to try and calm our neighbour.

"Well, then, Geoffrey Franklin?" said

Mrs Potter, trying to get her breath back. "You still think there's no need for a good guard dog at Picket Lake?"

"It was Cousin Eugene," sighed Grandad. "He's part of the family."

"A burglar in the family? Well, that's a fine state of affairs!" said Mrs Potter, heading home with her frying pan under her arm.

The dog spent a second night with us.

## Chapter 4
# The second Part of the Test

The next morning, Eugene came back to the house. He looked a bit tired, but he was very excited to share his great discovery with us.

"Canines have an extraordinary sense of smell!" he said, as he came in.

"What are you talking about?" asked Grandad.

"The canine's extraordinary sense of smell; that's the reason for last night's failure," explained Eugene. "The dog didn't bark because he recognised me, thanks to his 200 million olfactory cells."

"And what use will this incredible nose be to us?" asked Grandma.

"For all sorts of things, Aunt Margaret! Imagine that a friend of yours, or a relative, or even Arthur, got inconveniently lost in the woods. Your trusty guard dog would only have to give their clothes a sniff, and he'd bring them back to you, pronto!"

"Like a bloodhound," I added.

"Elementary, my dear Arthur!"

Grandma rolled her eyes. After the failed burglary, she needed proof. So Eugene kindly offered to pretend to get lost. He took off his jacket and handed it to Grandad, with a very serious expression on his face. Then he walked out the house, and we saw him hiding behind the stack of firewood.

"You'll have to go a bit further off, Eugene!" Grandma shouted out of the window.

He disappeared behind Mrs Potter's shed.

We waited a bit and then woke the dog, who was snoozing peacefully in the sun. Grandad held Eugene's jacket under the dog's nose and I shouted:

"Go for it, dog! Bring Eugene back!"

The dog ran off straight away. I was really pleased. He sniffed the grass... the old swing… the rowing boat… my duck… everything. He looked for Eugene everywhere. Then he set off down the little dirt track… and disappeared out of sight.

"Where's he off to now?" asked Grandma, a little anxiously.

"He'll be back. He'll be back," Grandad kept saying over and over. But he looked very nervous, too.

"What if he gets lost?" I asked.

"He won't, Arthur. He won't," Grandad reassured me.

"So what do we do now?" asked Grandma, annoyed.

Grandad didn't have time to come up with an answer. We heard a great cry of panic coming from Mrs Potter's garden.

"It's Cousin Eugene again!" I said.

"Oh dear," sighed Grandad.

We all ran over to Mrs Potter's garden. This time, she was pursuing Eugene with her garden hose.

"Would you stop watering him like that, Alison! That's Cousin Eugene!" shouted Grandma.

"Why was he hiding behind my shed,

then, eh? Was he going to steal my garden shears?"

"No."

"It's a family of bandits!"

Then I explained things to Mrs Potter.

"We were making the dog do a test, to see if he could bring back people who'd got lost."

"And where is this dog of yours?"

"We've lost him."

"Better and better," muttered Mrs Potter, walking back to her house.

Then the dog appeared through the

hedge, holding a rusty old tin can in his teeth. He came over and put it down at our feet. At least that was something.

"This dog really doesn't understand anything at all," sighed Grandma.

"So, you're not going to keep him?" I asked quietly.

"Now, now. Let's stay positive!" declared Eugene. "I'm sure we'll find a way this dog can be useful. We still have to do the final part of the Big Test!"

The dog spent a third night with us.

## Chapter 5
# The big Decision

Eugene came back the next morning, as he had promised. When he came in, he didn't say a word. He just took off his shoes, his socks and his shirt.

"What on earth are you doing, Eugene?" asked Grandma, wide-eyed.

"There's still one final stage of the test to do, Aunt Margaret. I'm going to simulate a drowning."

"Good heavens, Eugene! You aren't going to risk your life?"

"I have no doubt the dog will come and save me," said Eugene, bravely. "I'm sure of it."

"I must confess, a lifeguard would be really useful at Picket Lake," declared Grandma, glancing over at the dog, who was still asleep.

We woke him up, and we all went outside.

Eugene went down to the bank of the lake. He got into Grandad's rowing boat. He rowed for a while then he pretended to fall in, and went under. It was really good! Almost as good as his burglar impression!

"Heeeeeelp!" cried Eugene. "Heeeeeelp!"

As the dog wasn't watching, I gave him a bit of a shake.

"Off you go! Go save Eugene! This is your last chance. Show them how useful you can be!"

He lay down.

I heaved him back up.

He lay back down.

It was no use.

"Help! Heeeeeelp!" Eugene was still yelling. "I'm really drowning!"

We heard a huge SPLASH!

At first, we thought the dog had thrown himself into the water, and that he was going to save Eugene like a superhero. But no. He hadn't moved. It was Mrs Potter from next door who had dived into the water, and was swimming at full speed towards Eugene. She grabbed hold of his hair, helped him back into the rowing boat, and brought him back to us, safe and sound.

"The dog was a complete washout in the drowning test," said Grandad.

"What about me? Is no one going to thank me for saving him?" grumbled Mrs Potter.

"I'm enormously grateful to you, Miss Alison," said Eugene, through chattering teeth.

"Ha! Still…" muttered Mrs Potter.

Then Eugene came over to us and announced:

"Alas, I fear that this canine is absolutely no use whatsoever."

I hugged the big dog in my arms, and said:

"Maybe it doesn't really matter if he's useful."

"Arthur is right," added Grandad quickly. "After all, a dog is a dog." Eugene whispered to Grandma:

"In any case, with a neighbour like that, there's no doubt about it… you're completely safe!"

"Are you talking about me?" asked Mrs Potter.

"Of course not," said Grandad.

And to celebrate the big dog's arrival in the family, Grandma invited Mrs Potter round for dinner.

# ARTHUR

**Johanne Mercier**

It all started when this lady called Johanne thought about me in her head. Grandma said Johanne had written fifty-eight stories for children, and that one of her stories was made into a film. Grandma also said Johanne understands children because she used to be a teacher. But now she writes all day.

I think it must be really fun to write stories all day. When I grow up, I want to write stories like Johanne Mercier, and I also want to be a pilot. Grandad says there's nothing to stop me doing both, but I think that writing stories and flying a plane at the same time is not a good idea.

**Daniel Hahn**

Daniel Hahn translated the stories. He took my French words, and wrote them in English. He said it was quite a difficult job, but Cousin Eugene said he could have done it much better, only he was busy that day. So we got Daniel to do it, as he's translated loads and loads of books before. He also said he wrote the words for a book called *Happiness is a Watermelon on your Head*, but everyone else said that book was just plain silly.

Daniel is almost as clever as Cousin Eugene and he lives in England, in a house by the sea, with a lot of books.

**Clare Elsom**

I was so happy when we met Clare Elsom. She got out her pencils and pens and scribbled until the scribbles looked just like me! Grandma and Grandad said the resemblance was uncanny.

Clare has so many pencils and pens – at least twenty of them – and she spends all day drawing in lots of different books. I'm not sure that you are allowed to draw in books, but she seems to get away with it.

I like Clare because she likes egg on toast and exploring new places, and drawing me. But I think she wants my pet duck, so I will have to keep an eye on her.

More escapades with
Arthur coming soon

## Also available

ARTHUR

AND THE YETI

JOHANNE MERCIER

Arthur and the Guard Dog
ISBN: 978-1-907912-19-1

First published in French in 2009 under the title *Arthur et le gardien poilu*
by Dominique et compagnie, a division of Les Editions Heritage, Saint-Lambert,
Canada. This edition published in the UK by Phoenix Yard Books Ltd, 2013.

Phoenix Yard Books
Phoenix Yard
65 King's Cross Road
London
WC1X 9LW
www.phoenixyardbooks.com

1 3 5 7 9 10 8 6 4 2
A CIP catalogue record for this book is available from the British Library
Printed in China